For my father, Hugh Antonsen

The Big Sneeze/Mulberry/copyright page

Copyright © 1985 by Ruth Brown
First published in Great Britain by Andersen Press
Limited in 1985.

The Library of Congress has cataloged the Lothrop,
Lee & Shepard edition of *The Big Sneeze* as follows:

Brown, Ruth.
The big sneeze.
Summary: A farmer sneezes a fly off his nose and
causes havoc in the barnyard.
ISBN 0-688-04665-7 ISBN 0-688-04666-5 (lib. bdg.)
1. Children's stories, American. [1. Farm life—
Fiction. 2. Humorous stories] I. Title.
PZ7.B81698Bi 1985 [E] 84-23385

10 9 8 7 6 5 4 3 2 1
First Mulberry Edition, 1997
ISBN 0-688-15282-1

THE BIG SNEEZE

Ruth Brown

A Mulberry Paperback Book
New York

One hot afternoon, the farmer and
his animals were dozing in the barn. The
only sound was the buzz-buzz of a lazy fly.

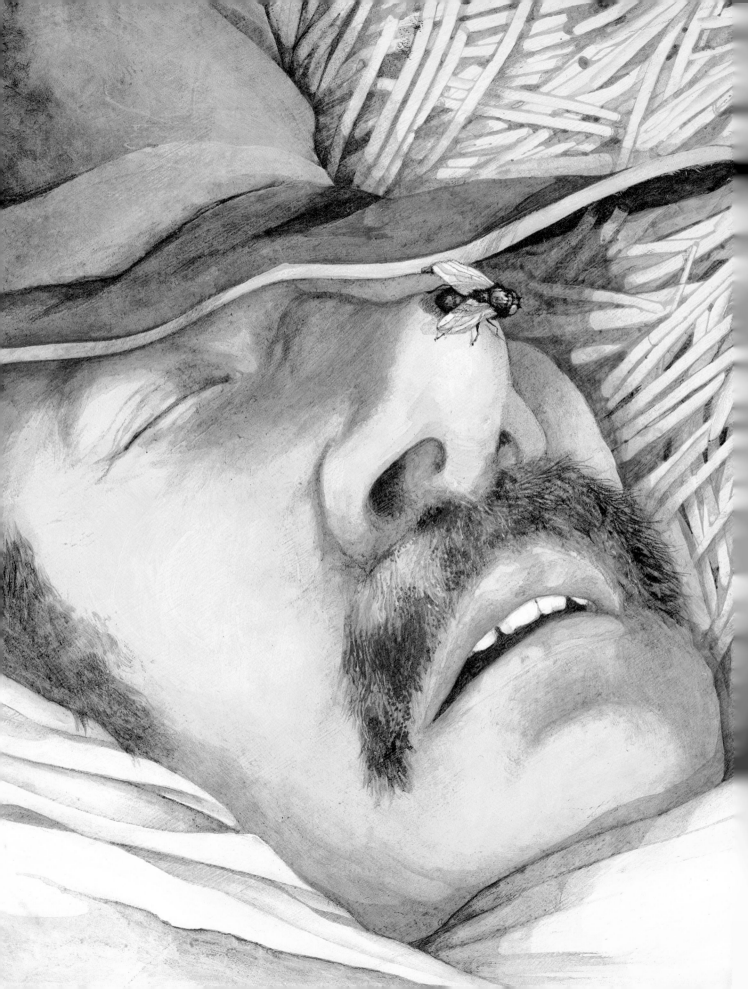

Suddenly the buzzing stopped –
the fly had landed right on the end of the farmer's nose!

"ATISHOOOOOOOOOOO!" the farmer sneezed so hard
that the fly was blown high up into a spider's web.

This disturbed the spider,
who captured the fly —

which alerted the sparrow,
who chased the spider.

This wakened the cat,
who leapt at the bird —

which woke the dog,
and frightened the rats –

who fled from the barn,
chased by the dog –

which scattered the startled
hens from their roost –

and panicked the terrified donkey!

"What on earth have you done?" shrieked the farmer's wife.

"Nothing, my dear," replied the farmer. "I only sneezed!"